PUFFIN BOOKS

The Toby Man

Tod Golightly has a lot to learn about becoming a highwayman, even though he is following in his father's footsteps. His first attempts at robbery are enthusiastic but markedly unsuccessful, and soon his dreams of gold and silver begin to fade – a decent meal is all he asks.

Then a wise old donkey, Matilda, offers her services and also introduces Tod to her friend Digby, a bull mastiff. Later they are joined by a ferret and a magpie – an unusual, but effective, band of robbers. Their first attack reaps rich rewards and Tod begins to dream once more of fame and fortune, a romantic picture of adventure and high living.

But he has reckoned without the Bow Street Runners, a group of trained detectives who easily outwit such an inexperienced robber. Surely Tod's loyal friends will find a way to help him? But what can a dog, a donkey, a ferret and a magpie do against the forces of law and justice?

Dick King-Smith was born near Bristol. After serving in the Grenadier Guards during the Second World War, he went on to spend twenty years as a farmer in Gloucestershire, an experience which inspired many of his stories. He went on to teach in a village primary school, and he had his first book published in 1978. Since then he has written a great number of books including *The Sheep-Pig* (winner of the Guardian Award), *The Mouse Butcher*, *The Fox Busters*, *Saddlebottom* and *Daggie Dogfoot*. He has also written four non-fiction books for Puffin: *Pets for Keeps*, *Country Watch* and *Water Watch*. He lives in Avon wi   ten
grandchild   vision

Other books by Dick King-Smith

———— • ————

The Toby Man

Dick King-Smith

Illustrated by Ian Newsham

PUFFIN BOOKS

PUFFIN BOOKS

Published by the Penguin Group
Penguin Books Ltd, 27 Wrights Lane, London W8 5TZ, England
Viking Penguin, a division of Penguin Books USA Inc.
375 Hudson Street, New York, New York 10014, USA
Penguin Books Australia Ltd, Ringwood, Victoria, Australia
Penguin Books Canada Ltd, 2801 John Street, Markham, Ontario, Canada L3R 1B4
Penguin Books (NZ) Ltd, 182–190 Wairau Road, Auckland 10, New Zealand

Penguin Books Ltd, Registered Offices: Harmondsworth, Middlesex, England

First published by Victor Gollancz Ltd 1989
Published in Puffin Books 1991
1 3 5 7 9 10 8 6 4 2

Printed by Clays Ltd, St Ives plc
Filmset in Monophoto Baskerville

Contents

Chapter One

Matilda

At the side of a muddy country road, a small footpad stood behind a large tree. The year was 1730, the night was wet and windy, and the small footpad was shivering, partly with cold, for his clothes were thin and ragged, and partly with excitement, for he was bent on highway robbery, for the very first time in his life.

Suddenly he heard the sound of footsteps squelching through the mud, and, peeping round the tree, saw the bent figure of an old woman approaching, supporting herself on a rough staff.

With pounding heart the small footpad stepped into the road, and cried (in as gruff a voice as he could muster), 'Stand and deliver!'

Tod Golightly came from a long line of robbers.

His mother's family were sheep-stealers, a high-risk

7

profession (more than one of them had dangled from a rope). But his father's people preferred to keep their feet more firmly on the ground. They were footpads to a man, working the toby – thieves' slang for the road – beside which they lay in wait to rob travellers. Robbery on foot was known as low toby, and Tod's father had advised him as to the conduct of it.

'Pick on the easy ones, son,' he told Tod. 'Go for the defenceless wayfarer – no sense in running risks. Never tackle a man on horseback – he'll ride you down. And as for carriages and coaches – steer clear of them. Holding up a coach is work for a mounted man – what we call high toby – like that there Richard Turpin up York way, with his fine black mare and his brace of pistols. 'Tis low toby for us footpads. No need for any of that "Stand and deliver" nonsense. Just sneak in quick and quiet, and away with whatever you can lay your hands on.'

'But Father,' said Tod, 'aren't you supposed to say "Your money or your life"?'

'Save your breath,' was the reply. 'Show 'em your knife. That'll do it.'

That was the last advice the footpad gave his son, for one very dark night shortly afterwards he sneaked in quick and quiet and showed his knife to a traveller, and – for the first and last time in his life – found himself staring into the mouth of a blunderbuss.

'Ah me!' said Tod's mother, drying her tears on a kerchief of fine Irish lace that her late husband had stolen from a passing pedlar. 'He's gone, my toby man. He did his poor best for us. Now 'tis up to you to take his place, Tod, and carry on the family tradition. The good name of Golightly is in your hands.'

As soon as Tod had uttered the words 'Stand and deliver!' he remembered that his father had advised him against such speeches. It did not matter, however, since the old woman plodded on past him without taking the slightest notice.

Tod ran after her and planted himself in her way.

Louder now he cried again, 'Stand and deliver!'

The old lady stopped and leaned on her staff. She stared at Tod, cupping one scrawny hand around her ear.

'Stand in the river?' she said. ''Twould make no odds if I did, young man – I be soaked to the skin as 'tis.'

Tod brandished his knife in her face. It was not a real knife, but he had carved it from a piece of wood and painted the tip of it red to make it appear blood-stained.

'Your money or your life!' he shouted.

'A funny sort of knife?' said the old woman. 'I should just think it is! Now stop thy games, there's a good boy, and stand aside.'

'But I'm a footpad!' said Tod.

'I can't help it if your foot's bad!' said the crone angrily. 'Thee'll have more than one bad foot if thee dussen't get out of my way!' and when Tod did not move, she raised her staff and brought the butt of it down on his toes.

As he hopped about in pain, she pushed past him, and, caught off balance, the small footpad toppled and fell with a splash into the roadside ditch.

'Hee-haw! Hee-haw! Hee-haw!' brayed a loud harsh voice above him, and, struggling to his feet, waterlogged, mud-covered and empty-handed, Tod saw a long-eared grey head sticking over the top of the hedge.

'Call yourself a toby man!' said the donkey. 'I know what I'd call you.'

'What?' said Tod wetly.

'I'd call you a silly ass.'

What happened next was, though he could not know it, to decide the whole course of Tod Golightly's future.

First, to fail miserably in an attempt at robbery, then to be ducked in a dirty ditch, and finally to be guffawed at by a donkey would have put most people off a life on the toby; most people indeed would have reacted angrily, cursing at fortune, swearing at the old woman, throwing stones at the animal; or perhaps they would have given way before the sheer unfairness of life, and have put their heads in their hands and wept; indeed for a moment Tod felt like having a good cry.

But then suddenly, as he fished his wooden knife from the water, the absurdity of it all struck him, and he began to laugh.

He laughed and laughed like a mad thing, standing knee-deep in the ditch, while the donkey stared at him with an expression of surprise on its mild hairy face.

'Oh Lord-a-mussy!' gasped Tod. 'A silly ass I may be, but you ain't! I'm grateful to you, my friend, that I am.'

'What for?' said the donkey.

'Why, for making me see the funny side of my first robbery. Now I can go home happy, thanks to you, even though I've stolen nothing.'

'You still could,' said the donkey.

Tod climbed out of the ditch and peered up and down the dusky road, but he could see no one nor hear the sounds of anyone approaching.

''Tis too late,' he said. 'No wayfarers will come now, they're all a-bed. There's nothing for me to steal.'

'Yes, there is,' said the donkey. 'Steal me.'

'Steal you?' cried Tod. 'But why do you want to be stolen? Aren't you happy as you are?'

'I am not,' said the donkey. 'I am either put to a cart and made to pull loads so weighty as almost to break my heart, or ridden by a man so heavy as almost to break my back, who beats me for going too slow or for stopping when I can go no further. And I get little to eat save thistles. Therefore I am not happy. You are looking for something to steal. I am looking for someone to steal me. There is no problem.'

'Well, there is one,' said Tod. 'What if I am caught? They hang folk for sheep-stealing, so for donkey-stealing I should think that I'd be hung, drawn and quartered.'

'But,' said the donkey, 'if you are not caught, think what you will gain. Such a lightweight would be a pleasure for me to carry all day long. Not for you the poor rewards of a footpad. With me as your steed, you could try your luck on the high toby!'

'I could?' said Tod.

I could! he thought.

I'll do it! he thought.

'I'll do it!' he said.

'Then listen to me, young master,' said the donkey. 'What do they call you, by the way?'

'T-Tod,' said the small footpad through chattering teeth, for he was very chilled from his soaking.

'I am Matilda,' said the donkey, 'and I am old enough to be your mother. You have a mother, I presume?'

'Y-Yes.'

'Then get you home to her, so that she may put dry clothes on your outside and some good hot broth in your inside, or else you'll have no need to worry about being hung, drawn and quartered. You'll catch your death of cold instead. Off with you now!'

'But what about you, Matilda?' said Tod. 'Aren't you coming? Where's the gate? I'll let you out.'

'Make haste slowly,' said Matilda, 'that's my motto. First you must be dry and fed and rested. Then you must bid farewell to your mother. Tell her that you are off to seek your fortune. Tell her you will return one day, laden with gold coins and jewels and gems and pearls and precious stones, enough for a King's ransom. Then come back. I will be waiting at dawn.'

Chapter Two

Digby

Dawn was breaking as Tod made his way back to the donkey's field. He was fed and rested, and now much better clothed. His mother had fitted him out with the best of his late father's spoils – a tricorn hat, a heavy fustian overcoat and a pair of stout boots. The coat reached almost to Tod's ankles, but the hat gave him a jaunty air as he strode along (awkwardly, for the topboots were so much too large that he had had to stuff rags into their toes).

He was so excited at the prospect before him that he did not feel in the least sad at leaving his mother.

'All this talk of what you will bring me,' she had said sadly. 'How do you expect me to believe that? Why, your poor father,' (and she shed a few more tears into the Irish lace) 'was a hard-working footpad all his life, and yet this kerchief was one of the few things of any value that he ever managed to steal.

Mostly it was paltry stuff – half a dozen eggs or a hen from a goodwife on her way to market, or a few coins from some old drunkard reeling home from the tavern. How could a lad like you bring me gold and jewellery as you say you will? To do that, you must rob the stage-coaches and the carriages of the gentry.'

'But that's what I aim to do, Mother!' cried Tod. 'Father may have been only a footpad, but I am going to be a highwayman!'

*

As Tod neared the donkey's field, he could see Matilda standing by the gate.

'Good morrow, Matilda!' he cried, hurrying to open it. 'Can we set out straightaway?'

'More haste, less speed, young master,' said Matilda, 'or all your dreams of high toby will come to naught. Whilst you slept, I have been thinking. Bold you may be, Tod, with your "Stand and deliver!" but folk will neither stand nor deliver anything to a lad with a wooden knife riding on an old donkey. A man must needs be frightened afore he hands over his purse. We need an ally, you and I, an ally whose very size and look will strike fear into any traveller, and I know of just such an animal.'

'Where?' said Tod.

'Here,' said Matilda. 'On this farmstead. Not half a mile hence. Up with you now, and we will go to him.'

'What animal is that we seek?' asked Tod as they trotted along, but Matilda only answered 'Wait and see', so Tod gave himself up to the novel pleasure of riding.

Sitting in the hollow of the old donkey's sway back, he found at first that his feet scuffed the ground, but he soon learned to bend his knees and grip with his thighs, holding lightly with one hand to Matilda's short stiff mane. In the other hand he held his wooden knife, and dreamed of deeds of derring-do.

16

Suddenly Matilda stopped.

Ahead of him, Tod could see a house, and a group of rough thatched farm buildings surrounding a yard. In the middle of the yard was a dog-kennel, and lying before it, at the end of a length of heavy chain, was the most enormous dog that Tod could ever have imagined.

'There,' said Matilda softly, 'is our ally. He belongs to the same man as do I, and has no more liking for him. As I have, he has suffered. Kindness he has never known, but beatings and kicks are two a penny.'

At that moment, with a rattle of his chain, the great dog stood up and shook himself.

'Lawks!' whispered Tod. 'What a size! Why, he's nigh as big as you, Matilda. What kind of dog is that?'

'A mastiff,' said the donkey. 'See his heavy body and strong legs and great feet, and that massive broad scowling face. Would he not frighten any wayfarer?'

'He frightens me,' said Tod.

'Never!' said Matilda. 'A toby man like you afeared of a dog!'

'He's a very big dog.'

'But he's chained up.'

'That's true,' said Tod with relief.

'And anyway,' said Matilda, 'he has a kindly nature despite his looks. But we don't want him to give tongue and rouse the household. Say first therefore that you are a friend of mine.'

Tod walked into the yard, leaving the donkey at the gate.

'I am a friend of Matilda's,' said Tod hastily, as the mastiff came out to the full length of the chain that was attached to the broad studded collar around his thick neck. He sniffed the air, and stared suspiciously from beneath wrinkled brows.

Now that Tod was close, he could see that the dog looked more sorrowful than fierce, and on an impulse he said, 'Don't look so sad.'

'Digby! Digby! Where are ye, ye brute? Wait till I catch 'ee, I'll beat the hide off of 'ee!'

But the only answer was the distant mocking bray of a donkey.

Chapter Three

Evil

By nightfall they had covered twenty miles.

'We must put as much distance as we can,' Matilda had said, 'between ourselves and possible pursuit,' and she plodded steadily along throughout the day, only stopping once for a drink at a wayside pond.

They went by lonely tracks and byways, and though they saw labourers in the fields, they met no one. Digby broke away from the others now and again, to lumber after rabbits that were far too speedy for him, and by the time the donkey called a halt, he was fairly dribbling with hunger.

Tod too was ravenous. Each time they came to a hill he would dismount – to save Matilda's legs – and snatch a few blackberries from the hedges, but at the end of the day he felt hungrier than he had ever felt in all his life.

'I could eat a horse!' he said.

'But not a donkey, I trust?' said Digby.

Matilda had chosen her stopping-place carefully, by a little hillside field at the edge of which stood a small rick of hay. Tod had opened the gate for her, and now she was munching away.

'There's a village in the valley below,' she said with her mouth full. 'Take Digby, and see what you can find to fill your bellies. But go privily, mind. None of your hold-ups, Tod, understand?'

'Yes, Matilda,' said Tod.

It was dark when they reached the village, Digby leading because his night-sight was much better and his sense of smell much much better than Tod's. And as they entered the village street, its shops and houses all already in darkness (for in those days folk went early to bed), the mastiff suddenly stopped and threw up his great head, sniffing in deep draughts of the night air.

'Aaaaah!' he growled softly. 'Fill your lungs with that, Tod boy!' and the spittle hung from his flews in ropes.

Everyone deserves a really lucky day now and again, and this was to be a lucky night for Tod and Digby. As Tod followed the questing dog, he too caught a whiff of the smell that was drawing Digby along as though he were being reeled in on an invisible line.

And what a smell it was!

Onions were in it and carrots and parsnips and turnips and potatoes, and meat was in it – thick-gravied, perfectly-cooked meat – and there was the scent of fruit in it. And topping everything off there was a hint, nay, more, a certainty, of beautifully baked and deliciously delicate flaky pastry!

'Digby, Digby, whatever is it?' whispered Tod, but the mastiff took no notice. He followed his nose until they came to a certain shop. Here he came to a halt and stood and stared through the lozenge-shaped panes of the lattice window, his long tail swinging steadily from side to side.

Tod had never learned to read, so the words above the window:

Jos. Morris-Pieman

visible in the light of a rising moon, meant nothing to him. But the smell was so strong now, even to his poor nose, that he was in no doubt about the nature of those shapes, rows and rows of humps and bumps, that lay beneath a chequered cloth on a long trestle table within.

Luck had brought them to a pie shop!

But how to get in?

'Go privily,' Matilda had said, so there must be no noise – of a smashed window, for example – to rouse the pieman and thus the villagers, and bring pursuit upon their heels.

Slowly, carefully, Tod lifted the latch of the shop door but it was bolted on the inside.

'Keep watch!' he whispered to Digby. 'I'll go to the back. There may be a way in there.'

Again Digby did not answer, so busy was he, snuffling at the lattice window. He was sniffing madly at one of the lower corners where the smell was strongest and most tantalizing, because, Tod could now see, a single lozenge-shaped pane was missing. But what use is that, thought Tod. I could get my arm through, but I couldn't possibly reach the window-latch.

At the back of the shop was another door, but that also was bolted, and a small window, but that was latched. There was also a lean-to shed, open-fronted, from which, Tod suddenly noticed, came a sharp rank scent as unpleasant as the pie smell had been delightful.

It came from a wooden cage, behind the bars of which, Tod could see, two eyes glowed in the moonlight. They were small eyes, set close together, and they were near to the floor of the cage. They were bright red.

'It's a ferret!' said Tod out loud.

The red eyes rose up as the ferret stood on its hind legs, peering out in a short-sighted way.

'It's a boy!' it said in a thin scratchy voice.

It was a dirty yellowy-white colour, and it was very long and low and snake-like, as ferrets have to be to get through small holes.

To get through small holes, thought Tod!

'What's your name?' he said.

'My name is Evil,' said the ferret.

'Look, Evil. Do you like meat pies?'

'You have a kind face,' said Evil, 'but apparently, few brains. The pieman does not waste his wares on me. Out rabbiting, he throws me the guts, and I may eat what rats I kill. But as for the pies, all I have of them is their smell.'

'Would you like one, now, tonight?' Tod said.

The ferret stared beadily at him with its bright red eyes.

'I should be your friend for life,' it said simply.

Tod opened the cage.

The rest was easy.

Once Evil had been slipped through the missing pane, the ferret snaked along the inner sill of the window and, standing up to its full height and scrabbling with its forepaws, succeeded in turning the latch. The window swung open.

In a flash Tod had clambered over the sill, tiptoed across the room, and whisked off the chequered cloth.

Oh what a sight was revealed!

There on the trestle table was the pieman's biggest baking of the week, all ready for market day on the morrow.

There were meat pies of every shape, round ones and oblong ones and neatly-folded pasties, and of every kind, pigeon pies, steak pies, mutton pies, game pies. And as well as meat, there was fruit – in tarts and puffs and flans and turnovers, apple and plum and cherry and strawberry.

Had the pieman woken in his bed upstairs (and luckily he slept heavily after his day's labours), he would have heard no sound but that of munching and swallowing, as boy and dog and ferret feasted.

Digby's appetite was of course the largest, and not till Tod had thrown him a dozen meat pies was the edge taken off it.

Evil ate the meat only from his pie, but the crust was not wasted for Digby had that too.

As for Tod, he bolted a couple of pasties and then set about the fruit tarts.

But, heartily as they ate, there was at last (which was when Digby could not manage another mouthful) still a great deal of food left on the table.

'We can't just leave all that,' said Digby, peering in through the window, his look even more than usually mournful at such a thought.

'We certainly can't,' said Tod. 'But how can I carry so much?'

'The answer is simple,' said Evil. 'Spread the table-cloth on the floor, place the food upon it, knot the corners of the cloth together, and you have a portable bundle.'

'Of course!' said Tod. 'How clever of you, Evil,' and he did as the ferret had suggested, piling together the remainder of the pies and pasties and tarts and puffs and flans and turnovers.

Then he went to the window to ask Digby to see that the coast was clear.

Then he knotted up his bundle, heaved it over his shoulder, and clambered out of the window.

'Goodbye, Evil,' he whispered, 'and thank you for your help,' but there was no answer to be heard or glint of red eyes to be seen, so Tod set off with his load.

A lucky day it may have been but it had also been a very tiring one.

Matilda was sleeping on her feet, standing beside the hay-rick, and Digby flumped down beside her. Tod managed to keep his eyes open long enough to hide his bundle in the hay, safe from prying animals of the night, and then he pillowed his head upon Digby's bloated belly and was asleep in a second.

When he woke next morning, his first thought was of the bundle of food (for he was already hungry again), and he pulled it out of the hay and began to unknot it.

Funny, thought Tod, the pies don't smell quite as good as they did.

He opened out the cloth, and there, slumbering peacefully in the middle of the pastries, was a very fat ferret.

Chapter Four

Loudmouth

'Evil!' gasped Tod, and at the sound of his voice Digby heaved himself to his feet. He came to look, wrinkling his nose. Then he bent his great head and carefully took the pie that was furthest from the ferret and chewed it moodily, while Tod recounted the night's adventures to Matilda.

'Clever of you to have thought of using the creature like that,' said Matilda, 'and fortunate that it seems to have decided to join our little band.'

'Why?' said Tod.

'Because,' said Matilda, 'you cannot count on raiding pie shops every day of the week. Such good fortune will not often come your way. But Evil here can be of the greatest help, to you and to Digby.'

'How? Why not to you?'

'Because,' said Matilda, 'I am a vegetarian. I can

find my food by the wayside. But you others need meat, and the ferret can provide it.'

'Rabbits, you mean?'

'Rabbits certainly, but poultry too. Think of all the hens and ducks and geese we shall pass on our journeys. Evil will be able to get into their sheds . . .'

'. . . and shed their blood,' said a thin scratchy voice. 'What an admirable idea. There will be eggs too. I am partial to an egg.'

'But how will Evil keep up with us?' Tod asked.

'The answer is simple,' said Evil. 'The donkey carries you, and you carry me. You have an overcoat with deep pockets. I shall be most comfortable and warm.' Tod looked a little doubtful, and Digby's melancholy face assumed an expression that was almost a grin, but Matilda said briskly, 'That's settled then. Now make your breakfasts, the three of you, and let us be off,' and she pulled a mouthful from the hay-rick.

While they were eating, they heard a sudden loud harsh noise, and a black-and-white bird flew down from a nearby tree and perched upon Matilda's back, flirting its long tail up and down.

'Spare a crumb for a starving widow!' cried the magpie to the pie eaters. 'Six children to support, poor little mites, and not a mouthful has passed my beak for days! Spare a piece of pie for a poor pie!' and she hopped down to the ground.

'Go away!' growled Digby, and 'Come nearer!' said Evil softly, red eyes gleaming, but Tod said, 'Poor bird! Have some of mine,' and he threw the magpie a lump of piecrust.

Matilda watched these reactions with amusement.

'You're too good-hearted, Tod,' she said. 'I don't know if we shall ever make a toby man of you.'

'But you heard what the bird said, Matilda!' cried Tod. 'She's lost her husband, she's got six little babies to care for, and she's starving!'

'She's something else too, Tod.'

'What?'

'A liar,' said Matilda. 'Magpies are not just thieves, you know. They tell lies about anything and everything. Never in all my long life have I heard the truth from a magpie.'

With a loud squawk of laughter the bird flew on to the donkey's back again. 'There's always a first time for everything,' she cried, and to Tod she said, 'The old moke is right. I have no husband to lose, I have no children to support, and my crop is full of worms and acorns. But that didn't stop me begging a few crumbs from a rich man's table.'

'Rich!' said Tod. 'You must be jesting! I have nothing but the clothes I stand up in, and my knife, and that's only made of wood.'

'You have more than that,' said Matilda quietly. 'You have a friend.'

'Two friends,' rumbled Digby.

'Three,' rasped Evil.

'Three friends!' screeched the magpie. 'And you say you have nothing! The truth is (the truth, mind, old moke) that you are indeed rich.'

'Yes, you're right,' said Tod, grinning happily. 'Friendship is worth more than all the jewels in the world.'

'Jewels?' said the magpie, cocking her head to one side.

'Tod has determined,' said Matilda, 'upon a life on the high toby. He plans to return one day to his mother laden with gold coins and jewels and gems and pearls and precious stones. He has me to carry him.'

'And me to protect him,' said Digby.

'And me to kill for him,' said Evil.

Once more the magpie hopped down from Matilda's back, and, keeping a wary eye on dog and ferret, walked over to Tod.

'None of your friends,' she said, 'can fly.'

Matilda stopped chewing.

'Tod,' she said slowly. 'This bird could be of use. She could fly ahead of us. To keep a look-out. For danger.'

'And for hen-houses,' said Evil.

'And for pie shops,' said Digby.

'And for carriages coming our way!' cried Tod. 'Carriages bearing rich gentlemen, their ladies dripping with jewellery!'

The magpie's black eyes twinkled.

'All that I could do,' she said. 'You have a steed and a guard and a provider. I could be your scout.'

'So you shall!' cried Tod. 'A splendid idea! Have some more pie.'

'Time we were afoot,' said Matilda, swallowing a final mouthful of hay, so Tod bundled up the few remaining pies, and Digby and Evil and the magpie licked and picked and pecked the last crumbs from the ground.

Then Tod put the ferret in his pocket, and called Digby, and closed the gate behind them, and hopped on Matilda's back.

'We go this way,' said the donkey to the magpie. 'Fly ahead and keep watch, bird. What shall I call you, by the way?'

'I have no name,' said the bird. 'Save that you have called me "thief" and "liar", old moke. What will you call me next?' and she gave a piercing shriek of laughter.

A little triangular head poked up under the flap of Tod's pocket, and a pair of red eyes regarded the magpie stonily.

'The answer is simple,' said Evil. 'We will call you Loudmouth.'

Loudmouth proved her worth before they had travelled half a mile. She came swooping back and perched above the others, chattering with excitement.

'Someone coming!' she cried.

'Man, woman or child?' said Matilda.

'It's a man, old moke,' said Loudmouth. 'A rough-looking fellow, all hung about with pots and pans, and pushing a handcart.'

'What's in the handcart?' asked Tod.

'Kettles, saucepans, all kinds of ironmongery,' said the magpie.

'A tinker,' said Matilda.

'A tinker!' said Tod scornfully. 'He'll have nothing worth the taking.'

'Tod, Tod,' said Matilda, 'use your brains. I told you, you cannot expect to live on a diet of pies. When Evil kills for you, fur or feather, will you eat it raw? He will, and Digby will, but you must needs cook it. What will you cook it in? How will you light a fire? You need some of that tinker's wares – a kettle, a frying-pan, a saucepan. And, what is more, you need what he must surely carry to do his work, to heat the solder for mending pots and pans – his tinder-box, his flint, and his steel. Your luck is holding. Just now you need to rob this man more than any rich merchant. Jump off now, and be about your work.'

'He's coming!' screeched Loudmouth from her perch.

'But where are you going?' said Tod anxiously to the donkey.

'We will not be far away,' said Matilda, and she and Digby disappeared into the shelter of a nearby thicket.

Tod stood in the road, and the tinker came into sight around the next corner. At first in the distance he seemed quite a small man, but the nearer he got the larger he loomed. He *is* a rough-looking fellow, too, thought Tod, and he was half minded to give the man good day and let him go on his way.

But what would the others think of me, he said to himself. I must be bold. After all, if the worst comes to the worst I'll wager I can run the faster.

So he drew his wooden knife and, trying to make his voice as deep as possible, cried, 'Stand and deliver!'

The tinker stopped and let go of the handles of his cart.

'You saucy varlet!' he said. 'Rob me, would you? Two can play at that game, my lad. Let's see what you have in that coat of yours,' and before Tod could move, the man grabbed him around the neck with one arm and plunged his other hand into Tod's pocket.

Then everything happened at once.

With a yell the tinker pulled out his hand with Evil dangling from its thumb, and as he danced about trying to shake the ferret off, Tod gave him a push and he tripped and fell. Before he could get to his feet, two huge paws were placed upon his chest, and his ears were filled with the rumble of a thunderous growl.

'Take everything!' cried the tinker. 'Take all I have. Only take this devil off my thumb and call off your monster of a dog!'

'I don't want all you have,' said Tod, when order had been restored. 'Just a kettle and a frying-pan and a saucepan.'

All these he found in the handcart, and a sack to put them in.

'Oh, and I shall need your tinder-box and your flint and your steel, I'm afraid,' he said, and, scowling, the tinker loosed a little leathern pouch from the belt of his jerkin and handed it over. Stuck through the belt, Tod noticed, was a sharp-looking knife.

'There's just one more thing,' he said, and he held out his hand. 'I'll have that.'

The tinker looked daggers at Tod as he slowly drew the knife, but Digby's growl was enough to make him hand it over.

'Thanks,' said Tod, and he in turn held out his old wooden knife with its red-painted tip.

'Fair exchange is no robbery,' he said, and Loud-mouth gave a squawk of laughter.

By now Tod felt sorry for the tinker despite his murderous looks, so he took out one of the remaining pies and gave it to the man.

As they rode away Tod looked back just before they turned the corner. The tinker was standing in the middle of the road staring after them. He shook one fist at them, blood still dripping from Evil's bite. In the other he held the pie.

'Let us hope,' said Matilda, 'that he decides to eat that pie soon. If he enters the village still carrying it, he is in for a rough reception.'

Chapter Five

To the Forest

For a week and more the robber band moved on across the countryside, and each day that passed found them more of a team. Each of them knew their duties, and as they became accustomed to one another, they began to appreciate their comrades' virtues and forget their vices.

Evil, for example, somehow did not seem to smell as bad once he was providing a regular supply of not only rabbits but also ground-nesting birds like partridges and quail. In fact the meat-eaters (of whom Loudmouth was one) ate royally, particularly one night when Evil killed, and Digby carried back, a brace of fat farmyard ducks.

Tod had soon mastered the art of fire-making, kindling the tinder with a spark struck by steel from flint, and then nursing and coaxing the flame with dry grasses and twigs until he had a good fire alight.

There were fallen branches aplenty for fuel, and no lack of water in pond or ditch to fill his cooking vessels.

Comfortably full of duck, Tod lay beside the fire and, in the flickering light of its flames, looked around at his four friends.

On a branch above him the magpie sat, silent for once.

Beside him the ferret curled luxuriously in the warmth, red eyes closed.

Opposite, the mastiff snored, heavy head resting on his massive paws, and twitched in his dreams.

And beyond the dog was the solid grey shape of the old donkey, asleep, as usual, on her feet.

What a lucky toby man I am, thought Tod, as he drifted towards slumber, to be the leader of such a band. But then he grinned to himself. The real leader, he thought, is Matilda. But where is she leading us?

'Where are you leading us, Matilda?' he said next morning as he rode along. 'We've been on the toby for almost two weeks and only robbed one wretched tinker. I'm not very proud of that, you know, or of stealing all the poor pieman's goods, or of trying to rob that old woman who pushed me in the ditch. I don't think I like robbing poor people. When am I going to rob the rich and start to make my fortune?

Why do we keep on and on? When are we going to stop?'

'Patience,' said Matilda, 'is a virtue. Trust me, Tod. I know where I am going.'

'How can you?' said Tod. 'So far from your home.'

'Every step I take,' said the donkey, 'brings me nearer home. We are heading for the place where I was foaled, country that I know like the back of my hoof. Soon we shall reach the town in whose broad High Street I was sold as a young jenny, on a market day many years ago.'

'And that is where we shall stop?' said Tod. 'In a town?'

'Not in the town,' said Matilda, 'but near to it. The first thing we need if you are to succeed as a highwayman is a highway, and through this town there runs a road along which travel the stage-coaches between London and Bristowe. The Great West Road they call it, and on it there will be coaches and carriages aplenty. And the second thing we need is a safe hiding-place from which to operate, a place where no man can find us.'

'And is that somewhere near this town?' asked Tod.

'It is. Above the town, and not a mile distant, is the forest called Savernake.'

'And this highway runs near it?'

'It runs through it,' said Matilda. 'Right through

the forest it goes, and the great trees line the sides of it
and join their arms high above it to make a long dark
tunnel. It is the perfect place for an ambush.'

Two days later, they struck the Great West Road.

'What's that strange hill there?' said Tod, pointing
ahead at a massive grassy tumulus shaped like an old-
fashioned beehive.

'That is called the Tump,' said Matilda. 'It stands
beside the road we seek. Not far to go now.'

'Glad to hear that,' grumbled Digby. 'We don't all
have horny feet like you, Matilda. My pads are sore.
I'll be glad of a rest.'

A little head appeared from Tod's pocket.

'Poor old Digby,' said Evil. 'Travel is so tiring, isn't
it?' and after an enormous yawn the ferret snuggled
back down again.

Loudmouth, who had been scouting in front of them
as usual, flew back now and perched on Tod's shoulder.

'There's a highway ahead,' she said. 'A busy one
too. Why, in the last ten minutes I have seen more
wheeled traffic than in all our journeying. I saw a fine
carriage-and-pair, what's more. Folk that own such a
turn-out must be well worth robbing. Think of their
gold watches and chains, their rings and bracelets,
their pretty sparkling baubles! Hurry, Tod, hurry,
do!' and off she flew again.

'Hurry, Matilda, hurry, do!' cried Tod, digging his heels into her sides, so keen was he to begin his real career on the high toby.

He could just picture himself riding out into the middle of the Great West Road, the tinker's razor-sharp knife in his hand, Digby at his side, grim and growling. Proudly he would sit astride his trusty charger, proudly he would cry in ringing tones, 'Your money or your life!' Fearfully the fat merchants and their wives would hasten to step down from their carriages and place their money and their jewellery upon the pieman's chequered cloth. Scornfully then the toby man would send them on their way and bundle up his booty. No more stealing of a few paltry pastries. He could buy enough pies to feed a regiment of cavalry.

'Hold your horses!' said Matilda sharply, stopping in her tracks. 'Have you never heard the saying "Untimely spurring spoils the steed"?'

'Oh you and your sayings!' cried Tod, and once again he dug his heels into the donkey's flanks.

The next moment he went flying.

Down went Matilda's head, up went her heels, and over her long ears sailed Tod, to land with a bump that knocked the breath out of him. And as he lay winded, Evil, angry at so rude an awakening, snaked out of his pocket and bit him in the leg.

'Ow!' yelled Tod, sitting up. 'Why did you do that?'

'The answer is simple,' said Evil. 'You upset me.'

'I upset you!' said Tod. 'Matilda upset me.'

'Which you deserved,' said Matilda. 'I did not ask to be stolen so that you could kick me as I used to be kicked. You need to mend your manners, Tod. You told me when we set out that your boots were too big for you. Now it is you who are too big for your boots.'

When any one of us gets a good telling-off, there are a number of ways in which we may react. We may feel anger in return ('Don't you talk to me like that!'), or self-pity ('It wasn't my fault!' or 'I couldn't help it!' or 'It's not fair!'), or we may simply sulk.

The hardest thing to do is what Tod now did.

51

'I'm sorry,' he said.

'That's all right,' said Evil. 'Put me back in your pocket.'

'That's all right,' said Matilda. 'Get up on my back again.'

Soft-hearted Digby said nothing, but he could not bear to see anyone else looking woebegone, so he gave Tod's face a thorough washing.

Half-drowned, but happy again now, Tod remounted his trusty steed, and they moved on towards the highway. Matilda stopped short of it, waited until the magpie rejoined them, and then addressed them all.

'The best thing to do,' she said, 'in my opinion, is to wait now till after dark when the road will be empty.'

'After dark, old moke?' said Loudmouth. 'But how shall I manage? I'm no fly-by-night.'

'You can ride,' said Matilda. 'I daresay I can manage the extra weight. But keep that loud mouth of yours closed if you please. I do not want us to be observed. We will make our way through the town and up to the forest. Then we can all get a good night's rest and see what the morrow brings.'

The old donkey turned her head to look directly at the toby man.

'After all,' she said mildly, 'there's no hurry, is there, Tod?'

'No, Matilda,' said Tod, grinning. 'Slow but sure wins the race.'

So they waited in the shadow of the huge grassy Tump until the last sounds of wheels and hooves and footsteps had died away and night had fallen. Then they made their way on to the Great West Road and turned eastwards.

The town was in darkness as they strode the length of its wide High Street, and those few dogs that came out to investigate retreated hurriedly at sight of Digby.

Beyond the last of the houses they crossed a bridge over a river, and began the long climb up a steep curving hill. And as they climbed, they saw on the skyline above, silhouetted against a rising moon, the arms of a thousand mighty trees waving a greeting.

'Journey's end,' said Matilda. 'It is the forest of Savernake.'

Chapter Six

The First Hold-up

At the top of the hill they left the road and pushed deep in among the trees, great beeches for the most part, that towered above them. Matilda led the band unerringly to a perfect resting-place, a deep grassy hollow ringed with thick bushes and roofed with a trellis of boughs, sheltered and secret and safe. Here they settled for the night, tired after their long journeying. Tod snuggled into a thick bed of dry beech leaves and slept like a log.

When he woke next morning, Matilda was grazing nearby.

'Where are the others?' he said.

'Evil and the bird are hunting in the forest,' said Matilda. 'Digby has gone to town.'

'Why?'

'He said he felt an urge to drop in at the butcher's.'

Tod felt his tummy rumbling.

54

'How lucky you are to have grass to eat,' he said. 'I'm almost hungry enough to eat some myself.'

'Come with me,' said Matilda, and she led him to some hazel-bushes heavy with nuts, and to a bramble patch full of blackberries, and to a little plot of mush-rooms.

'That's better!' said Tod after his breakfast, and then, 'What's that?' as there came to their ears a distant sound, a sharp clear sound, the rootle-toot-toot of a horn.

'Quickly,' said Matilda, 'follow me,' and she trotted off towards the high road.

'Where are you going – what's the matter – what was that noise?' panted Tod, running beside her.

'Post-horn – stage-coach – show you something – hurry,' puffed Matilda.

She made for the point where the road ceased to run level, at the very top, that is, of the steep hill, and here they hid in a thicket and waited.

Presently there was the sound of hooves, and there, trundling down the road towards them, was a big coach pulled by four big horses, and on the box above the rear horses or wheelers sat a big coachman, whip in hand, and by his side a big guard, yard-long brass post-horn in one hand, in the other an evil-looking blunderbuss.

'How am I ever to hold up that lot?' whispered Tod

to Matilda as the stage-coach rumbled nearer. 'The coachman will whip me, the guard will shoot me, the horses will trample me and the coach will run over me.'

'Wait,' said Matilda. 'Wait and watch.'

As the coach drew level with them, the coachman cried, 'Whoa then, whoa my beauties!'

He reined in the two leaders and they and the wheelers behind them came to a halt. A head poked out of the window of the coach, and a nervous voice called, 'Guard! Guard! Why have we stopped? Is it a highwayman?'

'Lor bless you, no, sir,' said the guard from his seat

on the box. He laid down horn and blunderbuss and jumped to the ground.

'I must needs put on the skid-pan, sir,' he said. 'The hill before us is a steep one,' and he busied himself fixing a heavy metal shoe against the rim of one of the rear wheels of the coach.

This done, the guard clambered back up on to the box. He raised the post-horn to his lips and blew another long rootle-toot-toot, a warning to some innkeeper in the town below to have food and drink ready, and a change of horses.

Then the coachman clicked his tongue and flicked his reins and touched the shoulder of the offside leader with his whip.

'Walk on steady now,' he said, and the stage-coach began its careful descent.

'Now do you see?' said Matilda.

'Yes!' said Tod excitedly. 'That's the time to strike! That's the only time to do it! The coach is stationary, the coachman has his hands full, the guard is off the box and unarmed! But how did you know, Matilda? How did you know the coach would stop there? How did you lead us to that sheltered place last night? How do you know exactly where to find nuts and berries and mushrooms?'

'I told you,' said Matilda. 'I am Savernake-born. My mother worked for a woodcutter here in the forest. That's how I know it so well. That's how I know that the London coach to Bristowe always stops at the summit of Forest Hill to put on the skid-pan.'

'Oh what a good idea of yours!' said Tod. 'Quickly, let us stop the very next coach!'

'"Good" and "Quickly" seldom meet,' said Matilda. 'First, there will be no other coach for two days. Second, we need the help of the rest of our band, of Digby in particular. And third, we must be well rested and, especially, well fed.'

'We shall be!' cried Tod. 'Look what's coming up the hill!'

Coming up the hill was Digby.

In his jaws he carried an enormous joint of beef.

A couple of days later, well rested and, especially, well fed, the toby man's band was ready. All knew exactly what to do.

Loudmouth was already sitting in the top of a hundred-foot-high Scots pine a mile away, her sharp eyes upon the east.

Digby was lying concealed in the roadside thicket at the top of the hill.

In the road, just below the crest of the hill, Tod sat astride Matilda.

All were alert. Only Evil slept peacefully in Tod's pocket.

Tod heard the distant notes of the post-horn at the
same time as he saw Loudmouth flying swiftly back
towards them down the long dark tunnel of trees.

'Five minutes!' she squawked. 'Coach'll be here in
five minutes.'

'Is the guard armed?' said Tod.

'Blunderbuss on the seat beside him,' said Loudmouth.

'We shall need you then. Stay close. Are you ready,
Digby?'

'Ready.'

'Remember, don't move until the skid-pan is fixed.'

Now there came the sound of hooves, and Tod and

Matilda moved slowly forward to breast the hill, timing things so that, as the coach drew to a halt, they were level with the nearside leader.

Off jumped the guard in front of them, and, as before, an anxious passenger wanted to know what was the matter, why were they stopping, was it a highwayman?

The guard smiled.

'There's not a living soul for miles around, sir,' he said, 'save for a lad on an old donkey, and if he be a highwayman, then I'm a Dutchman!' and, going round behind the coach, he knelt to attach the skid-pan.

'Now!' said Tod, and at his word, three things happened all at once.

From a low branch the magpie flew at the coachman and flapped about his head and screeched and chattered.

While he was thus distracted, Matilda drew level with the box, and Tod reached up and took the blunderbuss.

And out from the thicket came the great mastiff at a run, and knocked the guard flat, and placed his huge feet upon the man's chest, and stared down upon him with his customary doleful look.

Tod grinned at the guard.

'You're a Dutchman!' he said.

Then, bringing the blunderbuss to his shoulder, he pointed it at the door of the stage-coach, and cried, 'Your money or your life!'

Chapter Seven

The Biter bit

As the passengers – four men – hastily emerged from the coach, Tod called 'Leave him!' to the magpie, and to the coachman he said, 'Come down off your box, my good man.'

'Your good man!' spluttered the coachman, red-faced with anger, but the guard cried (indistinctly, on account of the weight on his chest), 'Do what he says, Joe, else I've no doubt this monster of a dog will tear my throat out!'

'He's right,' said Tod as the coachman got down. 'Do what I say, my good man, else I've no doubt this monster of a blunderbuss will blow your head off!'

Holding the short gun in one hand, he whipped off his tricorn and skimmed it at the coachman.

'Pass the hat round,' he said.

'These are not fine gentry,' he whispered in Matilda's long ear as the coachman went from one to another of the travellers. 'No rich pickings here, methinks.'

'Don't be too sure,' said Matilda. 'These are merchants by the look of them, that need to carry ready money for their business dealings.'

And indeed there was a very pleasant tinkling of coins as the first three men took their purses from their pockets and loosening the drawstrings, emptied a shower of money into the tricorn hat. But when the fourth passenger, a thin, mean-looking fellow, tipped up his purse, only a couple of coppers fell out. ''Tis all I have,' he said in a whiny voice. 'I spent the last of my money upon the coach fare. See, young sir, my pockets are empty,' and he turned the linings out of them.

'He has quite a pot-belly for such a skinny person,' murmured Matilda, and indeed there was an odd-looking bulge under the man's coat.

Tod put his hand in his own pocket and drew out Evil.

'Allow me to put my little friend here inside your coat, sir,' he said politely. 'If you speak the truth, why, you have nothing to fear from him. But if not, my little friend has very sharp teeth.'

Evil yawned, showing them, and the thin man hurriedly unbuttoned his coat. A large leather pouch that had been concealed within it fell to the ground with a satisfying thud.

Just then Loudmouth, perched on top of the stage-coach, cried, 'Horsemen at the foot of the hill!'

'Tip all that you have in my hat into that pouch, my good man,' said Tod to the coachman, 'and give them both to me.'

To Digby, still standing patiently upon the guard, he said, 'Let him up.' Then he ordered all six men into the coach.

Faced with the blunderbuss, they scrambled to obey, and when at last the boldest of them felt able to poke his head out again, the toby man and his band were nowhere to be seen.

Safely back in the grassy hollow in the depths of the forest, Tod spread out the pieman's chequered cloth (which he used variously as saddle, pillow or counterpane), and opening the leather pouch, emptied out the contents. Never had he seen so much money!

To be sure, some of the coins were only of copper – farthings and halfpennies; but there was a good deal of silver – silver pennies, twopenny and threepenny and fourpenny pieces, sixpences and shillings, half-crowns and crowns; and then there was gold – half-guineas, and guineas, and a number of two-guinea pieces. And to top it all, there was even a five-guinea piece, a large gold coin that bore the head of King George II, wearing a laurel wreath on his very long curly hair.

'A King's ransom!' gasped Tod.

'Hardly that,' said Matilda, 'but perhaps enough to ransom a knight, let's say, or a squire. Certainly more than you would ever come by honestly.'

Tod was not in the mood to worry about honesty.

'I expect the merchants got it by cheating people,' he said, and he began to play with the heap of clinking, chinking, jingling coins. The fact that the inscriptions upon them were all in Latin worried him not at all, since he could not have read them had they been in English; nor was he concerned about their total worth, since he did not understand their various values and had never learned addition. It was just a lot of money, a lovely lot of money!

After a while he found himself alone save for Loud-mouth. Matilda had gone to find grazing, Digby and Evil to try their luck with the forest rabbits. But the magpie was fascinated with the shining display. She would tap with her beak upon a coin (especially a gold one), and pick it up, and drop it again, and so to another, squawking and whistling with delight.

'What will you buy with it, Tod?' she said.

'Fine clothes!' said Tod. 'And a fine pair of jackboots that fit me. And a sword. And a brace of pistols. And a black velvet mask to hide my face. And a great ostrich plume to put in my hat.'

'And a fine horse to ride, I suppose?' said Loud-

mouth. 'Dressed like that, you'll surely not be content with an old donkey?'

'Oh no,' said Tod hurriedly, 'I couldn't do without Matilda,' but all the same a little imp of temptation whispered in his ear. He pictured himself galloping across the land, mounted on a magnificent fiery chestnut stallion. Dick Turpin would be no match for Tod Golightly, the terror of the toby, the scourge of the Great West Road!

Lost in his day-dream, he did not notice that when the magpie flew up into a tree overhead, she had something in her beak.

And the more Tod thought about all the fine things

he would be able to buy, the more he felt he must go quickly, now, before the others came back. Especially before Matilda came back, otherwise he felt sure she would think of reasons to stop him going.

'Wait a while,' she would say (probably adding one of her favourite bits of wisdom like 'Haste is from the Devil'). 'Wait till the fuss dies down. The news of the robbery will be all over the town. Everyone will be on the look-out for a boy on a donkey.'

Well, I shan't be on a donkey if I go now, thought Tod; and I can't take Digby anyway, for he'd be recognized, by the butcher as well, I daresay; and I can't take Evil for I shall need both pockets for the money – the pouch is no use, someone might identify it.

After more thought he left his tricorn hat behind, for the travellers would surely have made mention of that, and also his weapons, reasoning that an ordinary honest town-boy would not walk about with a razor-sharp knife stuck in his belt and carrying a blunder-buss. He filled his pockets with all the money and set out, trying hard, as he neared the town, to look like an ordinary honest town-boy.

In fact, he need not have worried.

The coachman, the passengers and, especially, the guard had agreed amongst themselves that, though they would report the robbery, they would alter the details of it somewhat. They could hardly tell the authorities that they had been held up by a boy on an old donkey. Rather it was, they said, by no less than three well-mounted heavily-armed highwaymen accompanied by a pack of giant dogs.

'I fought right valiantly, didn't I, Joe?' said the guard, showing the bruises on his chest where Digby had stood on him. 'But they was too strong for us.'

So no one, had Tod but known it, was looking for him as he made his way cautiously towards the centre of the town, by way of narrow alleys and side-streets rather than along the main thoroughfare.

The nearer he got, the more he wished he had not come. What he had said to Loudmouth had been foolish. How could he possibly just march into shop after shop and buy clothes and boots and sword, pistols and mask and ostrich plume! They would take one look at him in his dirty heavy old fustian overcoat and his wayworn outsize boots and say, 'And where did you get all that money, my lad?'

Tod put a hand in each pocket to reassure himself that it was still there, and it clinked and chinked and jingled most pleasantly. Then he felt someone grasp his collar from behind and heard a voice in his ear.

'And where did you get all that money, my lad?'

said the voice, in most unpleasant tones. 'I'll have it, or I'll have your life!'

'There wasn't anything I could do,' said a penniless Tod miserably to Matilda that evening. He picked up Evil and put the ferret in his pocket, empty again now. 'He was a great hulking brute,' he said, 'and he shoved me into a dark doorway and put a dagger at my throat and took the lot.'

'Fancy!' said Matilda solemnly. 'Robbed by a common footpad!'

'It was downright dishonest of him!' said Tod.

For the second time since they had met, he felt like having a good cry. Then he caught Matilda's eye, rolling comically, and once again he began to laugh at the absurdity of it all.

'Ha! Ha! Ha! Ha!' roared Tod, and 'Hee haw! Hee

71

haw!' brayed Matilda, while Digby sat and stared gloomily at the pair of them.

'Oh Lord-a-mussy!' gasped Tod at last, wiping his eyes. 'Just think,' he said to the magpie who was perched upon his shoulder, 'this morning I was a rich man. Now I haven't a farthing! What d'you think of that, eh?'

For answer Loudmouth fluttered up into the tree above, poked her head into a hole, and flew down again. In her beak was a large gold coin that bore the head of King George II, wearing a laurel wreath on his very long curly hair.

Chapter Eight

'I only want change'

'**Y**ou may not have a farthing,' said Matilda, 'but you still have a deal of money. That coin would be half a year's wages to a labourer. You must change it.'

'Change it?' said Tod.

'For smaller coinage. Just imagine what a baker would say if you offered him this for a loaf of bread. And we don't want to keep all our eggs in one basket.'

'Bakers don't sell eggs,' said Tod, puzzled.

'Listen,' said Matilda. 'If you exchange this gold piece for silver and coppers, then when you go to a shop you need take only a few coins. You will not arouse suspicion and you will not lose much should you be robbed again. The rest we can hide somewhere.'

'In the hole in the tree!' squawked Loudmouth. 'There's plenty of room in there, and no one could reach it, except me. I could store it all there for you and fetch it down when you needed it, easy as pie!'

Digby looked more than usually worried.

'How can he change the coin?' he rumbled. 'Folk are bound to wonder how he came by it.'

'And even if a shopkeeper would oblige,' Tod said, 'how am I to know he gives me fair value? What is to stop him cheating me?'

A triangular red-eyed face poked out of his pocket.

'The gun,' said Evil. 'Point the gun at him and then see how honestly he will treat you.'

'But I cannot walk into the town carrying a blunder-buss,' said Tod.

'Evil is right,' said Matilda thoughtfully. 'You had better make use of the gun. And you are right. You must not take it into town. Therefore it follows that you must use it out in the country, on some lonely road.'

'Hold up another coach, d'you mean?' said Tod.

'Not yet awhile. They will be searching for us. This is something you must do without me. It's back to the low toby for you,' said Matilda.

So, next morning, Tod lay concealed in a dry ditch by the side of a lonely track deep in the forest of Savernake. In his hand was the blunderbuss, in one pocket the five-guinea piece and the ferret.

'I must take Evil,' he said to Matilda. 'Then if anyone tries to rob me again, he'll wish he hadn't.'

'A pedlar,' said Matilda, 'would be as good as any. They carry money for their trading. And if he hadn't enough, you could always take goods instead. He'll have a laden packhorse or two behind him.'

But no pedlar came in sight that morning. Not a living soul came in sight in fact, nor was there a sound to be heard save for occasional bird-song and the small snores of Evil.

By early afternoon Tod was about to give up, when he heard the noise of hooves on the rough stony path. Coming slowly towards him was a man mounted on a grey cob. The man – a tall thin elderly man, Tod could now see – was dressed all in black; black coat and breeches and stockings and brass-buckled shoes, and he wore a grey peruke or wig under a black high-crowned hat.

'Never tackle a man on horseback – he'll ride you down,' his father had said to him, but surely this one would not? Tod had never in his life been inside a church, but he knew a parson when he saw one, and he was seeing one now.

He looked carefully as the rider drew near and noted that, as might have been expected, he wore no sword. More, he had a very gentle face, a face no longer young certainly but the lines upon it spoke of laughter, not of frowns.

Tod did not feel that he could possibly point a gun

at so kindly-looking an old man, so he left it in the ditch and stepped out on to the track.

The parson drew rein.

'Give you good day!' he said, smiling and raising his high-crowned hat in greeting.

What a nice man, thought Tod (who had never met one before). I'm glad it's only fair exchange I'm bent on and not robbery, and he took off his tricorn and made a little bow and said, 'Good day, sir.'

He put his hand in his pocket and, from beneath a sleeping Evil, extracted the five-guinea piece.

'I wonder,' he said politely, holding it out, 'would you have the goodness to change this for me?'

The parson took from his breast-pocket a pair of eyeglasses and fitted them on the bridge of his nose. Then he took the coin from Tod's hand.

'Great Heavens!' he said.

Then he clambered down from the cob, threw the reins over her head, and gave her a slap on the rump, saying, 'Go and find yourself some grass, Martha.'

He sat down upon a convenient fallen tree-trunk and beckoned Tod to sit beside him.

'What is your name?' he asked.

'Golightly, sir. Tod Golightly.'

'Mine is Appletree. Parson Appletree. Now, Tod Golightly, do you know what this is?'

''Tis a gold coin, sir,' said Tod.

'It's a five-guinea piece,' said the parson, 'the most valuable coin of His Majesty's realm. See what is written around the royal head,' and he held it out to show the inscription:

GEORGIUS II DEI GRATIA

'I cannot read. Nor write,' said Tod.

'Do you know your numbers?'

'No, sir.'

'Then, if I am to give you change for this coin, how will you know that you receive fair value? What is to stop me cheating you, Tod?'

'Point the gun at him,' Evil had said, but Tod was more sure than ever that he could do no such thing to this man. There was no need anyway. Of course he would not cheat him.

'Of course you would not cheat me,' he said.

'Why? Because I am a parson?'

'No, sir. Because you are an honest man, it's plain to see.'

'And are you an honest boy?'

'Oh yes, sir!' said Tod.

'Then tell me honestly. How came you by this five-guinea piece?'

'I stole it,' said Tod.

Parson Appletree pursed his lips, looking at Tod over the top of his eyeglasses.

'You are no liar,' he said. 'Why did you steal it?'

'Thieving is my profession, sir,' said Tod. 'I come from a long proud line of thieves, sheep-stealers on my mother's side, and footpads on my father's. A footpad all his life, my father was.'

'Was?'

'He met with a bit of bad luck,' said Tod. 'But he'd have been pleased with me if he had lived, for I'm on the high toby, you see, sir! One day I shall return to my mother laden with gold coins and jewels and gems and pearls and precious stones! I'm a highwayman, I am! And the leader of a band of robbers!'

'Yet you are offering me this gold coin in exchange? Surely a highwayman would keep it, and take my purse as well? And maybe my horse into the bargain? I am an old man and you are young and strong. I could not stop you.'

'Oh bless you, no, sir!' said Tod. 'I only want change, that's all. I'd be much obliged.'

Parson Appletree took out his purse and counted the money in it.

'I fear there is not enough,' he said. 'Country parsons are not the wealthiest of men.'

'There look to be a great many coins there,' said Tod. 'That will be enough to be going on with, I'm sure.'

'There is no more than two guineas in all,' said the parson. 'Less than half the value of your coin.'

'Take it, sir,' said Tod, holding out the five-guinea piece. 'Perhaps I could have the rest later. I could come to your house if you will tell me where you live.'

'That would indeed be pleasant, Tod,' said Parson Appletree, smiling. 'I have never before played host to a highwayman. A mile or so up this track there is a village at the edge of the forest. The parsonage stands beside the church.' He got to his feet and gave a whistle and the grey horse Martha came to it.

Once mounted on the stocky cob, his long legs dangling, the parson looked down at the toby man.

'You would not wish me to preach you a sermon,' he said, 'but I beg you to give some thought to the eighth commandment.'

'Sir?'

'"Thou shalt not steal". That is what is written in the Good Book. Can you not stop?'

'I've only just started,' said Tod.

Parson Appletree gave a small sigh and a big smile at the same time.

'At any rate be sure to come and visit me, Tod Golightly. I should much like to see you again. And I am of course in your debt to the tune of three guineas.'

'I'll come, sir!' cried Tod. ''Pon my honour I will!'

He stood in the forest track, watching horse and rider

grow small in the distance. Once the parson turned in his saddle and waved, and Tod waved back. Then they were lost to sight.

He's going home, thought Tod, and for the first time since he had left it, he began to muse about his own home, far away. To be sure, it was not much more than a hovel, but it was cosy and warm (he imagined his mother sitting by the fire, waiting) and there was a comfortable bed in his little room. Here he had no bed but the ground and no roof over his head but the forest canopy. A lump came into his throat and he gulped and sniffed.

The ferret's face appeared from his pocket, yawning.

'What ails you?' said Evil.

'I've got a bit of a cold,' said Tod.

'I never get colds,' said Evil smugly. 'It's drinking blood that keeps me so fit,' and he snuggled back down again.

'Courage, Tod,' said the toby man to himself. 'It's high time for another hold-up. The sooner I can make my fortune, the sooner I shall see mother again.'

He wiped his nose on his sleeve. Then he picked the blunderbuss out of the ditch, sloped it over his shoulder, and marched off through the trees to rejoin the others.

Chapter Nine

The Second Hold-up

Savernake Forest was home to the red deer. Already Tod had seen numbers of them grazing amongst the trees or reaching up to the lower branches to browse on twigs and bark, but he could never get near them. At sight of him – particularly if Digby was with him – they would hurry away with long swinging strides.

Now, suddenly, as he made his way back from his meeting with the parson, he caught a glimpse of something moving in a little clearing ahead.

Carefully he crept forward, keeping a huge beech between the animal and himself. He reached the tree and peered around the trunk.

There, not much more than a stone's throw distant, was a magnificent red deer stag!

Look at his antlers! Tod thought. And the size of the creature! Why, there was enough meat on him to feed them all (except Matilda) for weeks! And not just any old meat, but venison, the food of kings! Doubtless King George ate venison for breakfast every day!

Tod did not know that red deer everywhere were the King's beasts, and that to kill one was a terrible crime. All he knew was that here he was – with a loaded weapon – and there was a stag.

He raised the blunderbuss.

If Tod had ever fired a gun before, things might have been different. First, he would have known that the discharge of it causes a recoil, especially the discharge of a blunderbuss, designed to throw a heavy spread of metal – shot of all sizes and even nails – and primed with a generous measure of powder.

Second, he would have known that, to minimize the shock of discharge, the butt of the gun must be pulled hard into the firer's shoulder.

And third, he would have known that anyway the stag was beyond the range of a close-quarter weapon like his.

He knew none of these things. He pressed the trigger, and the blunderbuss went off with a mighty roar and knocked him flat on his back.

For a moment he lay dazed, and, when he came to his senses, it was to see a pair of red eyes peering short-sightedly into his own.

'What have you shot?' said Evil in his thin scratchy voice.

Tod sat up and looked around. Of the stag there was no sign.

'Nothing,' he said, 'but I've only just realized – I've no way of loading the thing again. What shall I do?'

'The answer is simple,' said Evil. 'You merely pretend that it is loaded. People will not know, and so be just as frightened.'

'It feels as though Matilda had kicked me,' said Tod, rubbing himself gingerly. 'If you knew how my shoulder is aching, you would be sorry for me, Evil.'

'It is you who should be sorry,' said Evil sourly. 'My head is ringing like a tocsin. It is a great mercy

that you will never be able to fire that contraption again.'

'You're angry with me,' said Tod. 'Aren't you?'

'The answer is simple,' said Evil. 'Yes.'

'Are you angry with me?' said Tod to Matilda that night.

They alone of the band were awake beside the embers of a fire that Tod had made within the grassy hollow. He had told of the day's happenings, of his meeting with the parson (in which Matilda seemed interested), and of his attempt to shoot the stag (which made Digby dribble sadly at the thought of so much lost meat). Loudmouth had taken much pleasure in storing all the silver and copper coins in the tree-hole, and Evil had curled up in a ball and gone to sleep in a bad temper.

'Angry?' said Matilda. 'No, why should I be?'

'Well, I don't seem to be having much success. In making my fortune, I mean. It's high time for another hold-up, don't you think?'

*

'It's high time for another hold-up, don't you think?' they said to one another at the London offices of the stage-coach company.

'This gang that's operating in Savernake Forest, for example – three well-mounted heavily-armed high-waymen, accompanied by a pack of giant dogs, they say.'

'We must protect our passengers.'

'We must meet force with force.'

'At least six strapping men.'

'All armed to the teeth!'

'But if they ride on the outside of the coach, the gang will see them and be warned and remain in hiding rather than risk a pitched battle.'

There was a pause, and then someone said, 'All that is true – if our men ride on the *out*side of the coach.'

So it came about that, some days later, Loudmouth came flying back from her look-out perch on top of the hundred-foot-high Scots pine, bringing with her news that was not quite accurate.

'It's unguarded!' she screeched as she landed beside the rest of the band, waiting concealed in ambush at the same spot at the top of Forest Hill. 'The westbound coach is unguarded – just the coachman on the box and no sign of a weapon beside him!'

'That should make things very easy,' said Matilda. 'Let us change the plan. The coachman will have to put on the skid-pan himself. Let him do so, Tod, and allow him to climb back on to the box, and then cry your "Stand and deliver" to the passengers. They will do just that, in the face of the blunderbuss. Make them throw their purses to you and then send them on their way.'

'Better if I went with him,' growled Digby.

'No need,' said Matilda. 'It will be simple.'

'In sight!' squawked Loudmouth, and 'Ready?' said Matilda and 'Ready,' replied Tod.

'Whoa now!' cried the coachman to his horses as the coach rumbled up, and when it came to a stop, he got down and set about fixing the skid-pan. This done, he climbed back on to his box.

'Watch out, my good man,' said Tod under his breath. 'Here comes Tod Golightly, the terror of the toby, the scourge of the Great West Road,' and he stepped out of hiding, gun in hand, and cried in ringing tones, 'Stand and deliver!'

The coachman dropped his reins and raised his hands above his head. The passengers however did not seem inclined to emerge.

'Your money or your life!' shouted Tod. 'Out you come now, all of you, and look sharp about it!' and at that, the coach door flew open and out leaped six strapping men, all armed to the teeth!

Chapter Ten

'It's the rope!'

It is doubtful whether, had the blunderbuss been loaded, Tod would have had time to fire it, so quick were the Bow Street Runners. For these were the men that the stage-coach company had chosen to employ – trained detectives whose job it was, in those days before England had a proper police force, to find and arrest criminals. From their headquarters in Bow Street in London they operated as a rule on foot, hence their name. But this day they had been carried to their work, and they went about it with professional speed.

In the twinkling of an eye Tod found himself flat upon the ground, with one Runner sitting upon his chest while another had ripped the blunderbuss from his grasp. Of the other four, two covered him with drawn pistols while two stood guard, facing east and west, in case the highwayman had accomplices who might come to his help.

But of Tod's accomplices, three at any rate were helpless.

Matilda saw this immediately from their place of hiding, and spoke quickly to Digby. The great mastiff's hackles were up and terrible growls rumbled in his throat as he saw his master overpowered, but Matilda said urgently 'No, Digby! Stay still! Keep quiet! If you try to save him, they will shoot you down.'

'Like a dog,' added Loudmouth.

'But we can't just let them take him,' snarled Digby.

'We can't stop them,' said Matilda.

'Listen,' she said to the magpie. 'They will throw him in the coach and take him down into the town, to the gaol. Follow and find where it is, and then fly back to us. We will wait at the hollow.'

But before the Bow Street Runners did throw Tod into the coach, the man who had been sitting on him suddenly jumped up with a yell, clapping his hand to his backside.

'He bit me!' he cried. 'The fellow bit me!'

'Fellow!' said the others, now that they could see Tod plainly for the first time. 'Why, he's only a bit of a lad!'

One of the Runners pulled Tod to his feet.

'Just what d'you think you're playing at, my boy?' he said.

Though Tod was by now very frightened, he kept

his head. If they think it's only a game, he said to himself, perhaps they'll just give me a good cuff and let me go.

'Please,' he said, 'I was playing at being a highwayman.'

Another Runner picked up the blunderbuss.

'And where did you get this?' he said.

'Please,' said Tod, 'it fell off the front of a stage-coach,' and at that the man who had been bitten did give him a good cuff. But they didn't let him go.

'Tie him up,' said one, and 'Not worth the rope,' said another. 'He'll give us no trouble.'

'It's the rope for him anyway,' said a third Runner, 'once he's been before the Justices. Then he'll never trouble anyone again.'

Tod gulped.

'What do you mean, "It's the rope"?' he said in a choked voice.

'Round your neck,' said the man, 'with the other end over the gibbet. That's the penalty for robbery on the King's highway – hanging!' and then they threw him inside and jumped in after him, shouting to the coachman to drive on.

Behind the coach, stopping every now and then to perch in the hedges, for the braked progress down Forest Hill was a slow one, there flew a solitary magpie.

*

The cell in the town gaol was narrow and dark, with nothing in it but a rough wooden bench to serve as a bed. There was one little window, set high in the wall, much too high for Tod to reach let alone see out of it.

The toby man sat on the bench with his head in his hands. Once again, and this time for the best of reasons, he felt like having a good cry, and this time there was nothing absurd in the situation for him to laugh at. There was nothing to laugh at at all.

But before the tears started to flow, he heard a familiar squawking voice, and, looking up, saw Loudmouth's beak poking in at the window.

At the same time another face appeared out of his pocket, yawning hugely.

'Where are we?' said Evil.

'In gaol,' said Tod in tones of deepest gloom.

'Don't worry,' said Loudmouth cheerfully. 'I followed you and now I can tell Matilda and Digby where you are. They'll get you out.'

Evil looked round the little cell reflectively.

'An easy matter,' he said sarcastically, 'for a dog and a donkey to burst into a gaol, and turn the key and draw the bolts of this cell door (with their teeth, I presume?) and rescue our friend here, while the gaoler (one supposes) stands idly by. An easy matter.'

He slid out of Tod's pocket and began to explore the limits of the cell.

'Matilda will think of something,' said Loudmouth. 'I'll go to her now.'

'Wait,' said Tod.

Evil is right, he said to himself, Matilda and Digby cannot help me. It needs another human being to get me out of this place. But I know no one.

Then he jumped to his feet in excitement. I do know someone, he thought, someone I'm sure would help me somehow, if only I could get word to him!

'Wait,' he said again to the magpie, and sat down, thinking hard.

How could he send word when he had nothing to write with, nothing to write on? Even if he had, he had never learned to write. Even supposing that he had pen and paper and ink and had been able to write a letter, how could he make use of Loudmouth as messenger when he could not reach the window to give her the message? He looked round the cell for inspiration but it was bare. Evil had vanished.

At that moment the ferret reappeared out of a small drain-hole in one corner.

'One of us can escape, at all events,' he said.

And then a ready-made plan flashed into Tod's mind.

'Don't go yet, Evil,' he said. 'Hide yourself back in that drain for a while,' and he went to the cell door and banged upon it.

After some time the spyhole in the upper part of the door slid open, and the turnkey peered in.

'What ails you, boy?' he said.

'Please,' said Tod. 'Please could you allow me pen and paper?'

'What for? What tricks are you up to?'

'I only want to write a letter to my mother, to tell her what has befallen me. She is a widow, sir, and I am her only child.'

Perhaps it was because the turnkey had a son of about Tod's age or perhaps it was simple kind-heartedness, but with much grumbling he fetched paper and quill and ink, and unlocked the door and handed them in.

'Thank you, thank you!' said Tod, and, waiting till door and spyhole were closed, began slowly and carefully to draw a picture upon the sheet of paper.

'Evil,' he called softly as he drew, and the ferret came out of the drain. 'When I've finished,' said Tod, 'take this in your mouth and go outside and give it to the bird,' and to Loudmouth he said, 'Fly quickly with the paper to Matilda. She will understand what I mean, I hope and trust.'

Though Tod could not write a word, not even his own name, he could draw a bit, and it was quite plain, before he folded it across and across into a neat package, what the finished picture was.

The Toby Man

Within a circle was the head of a man, a man with a straight nose and a full chin and rather bulgy eyes, a man who wore a laurel wreath on his very long curly hair.

Chapter Eleven

Parson to the Rescue

By the time Loudmouth reached the grassy hollow the short winter's day was nearly over. In the twilight Matilda and Digby peered down at the piece of paper. Neatly, with beak and claw, Loudmouth had opened the folded sheet and spread it before them.

Digby looked not only sorrowful as usual but puzzled, his brow a mass of wrinkles, but Matilda said immediately, 'The five-guinea piece.'

'Tod said you would understand,' said Loudmouth.

'I do,' said Matilda. 'He needs help.'

'What help will a five-guinea piece be to him now?' said Digby. 'If he is locked up, how can be spend it?'

'He does not need the money,' said Matilda. 'He needs the man who changed it for him.'

'The parson!' cried Loudmouth.

'But how are we to find him?' asked Digby.

'I know that village on the edge of the forest,' said

Matilda. 'My mother used to go there carrying pannier-bags filled with firewood, with me trotting at her heels. I can find the parsonage.'

'Clever old moke,' said the magpie.

'Let us go now,' said Digby, but Matilda, as usual, was not to be hurried.

'"Haste trips up its own heels",' she said. 'We will go at dawn.'

And so next morning three figures could be seen approaching the village at the edge of the forest. On Matilda's back perched Loudmouth, in her beak the message which she had neatly re-folded, while Digby brought up the rear. Along the village street they went, and there beside the church stood the parsonage. Before the parsonage was a paddock, over whose rails a stocky grey cob looked with interest at them.

Matilda stopped.

'Pray tell me,' she said politely, 'does Parson Appletree live here?'

'He does,' said Martha.

'He is a kind man to his fellow humans,' said Matilda. 'That I know already. Is he also well disposed towards animals?'

'None more so,' said Martha. 'Like Saint Francis of Assisi, he is friend to all the beasts of the fields and the birds of the air. No need of words to tell him the reason for your visit. Whatever it is you want, he will know.'

*

Parson Appletree was sitting at his breakfast when he heard the knocker of the front door go tap-tap. As he went to open it, he saw that whoever had knocked had pushed a folded piece of paper through the slit of the letter-box. He picked it up and unfolded it. Then he took his eyeglasses from his breast-pocket and fitted them on the bridge of his nose, and studied the drawing for a moment before opening the door.

Outside, on the crescent of gravel before the parsonage, there stood an old grey ass with a mild hairy face, and beside it a great brindled mastiff. On the donkey's back perched a black-and-white pie, flirting its long tail up and down.

As soon as it saw the parson, the magpie flew away, calling loudly in its raucous voice, and perched on the paddock rails, and flew back, and then away again, calling all the time.

Parson Appletree walked forward, smiling his gentle smile, and laid one hand upon the donkey's head, fondling the roots of her long ears with skilled fingers, while with the other he patted the dog who wagged half his great body from side to side and dribbled with pleasure at the touch.

'I think,' said the parson, 'that you must be the band of that great highwayman Tod Golightly. I think that he is in some sort of trouble. I think that he needs me. Maybe it is only for his three guineas change, but more likely, I think,' he said as Loudmouth flapped frantically before his face, screeching with impatience to be gone, 'that it is a more serious matter.'

He gave a whistle, and when the cob came to the paddock gate, he opened it and said, 'Go you to your stable, Martha. I will be with you in a moment to saddle up.' Still holding the gate open, he said to Matilda, 'Pray come in here and rest awhile, my dear, while your friend the bird takes me to your master. Your other friend here shall guard my house during my absence, if he will be so good.'

'Parson's out betimes today,' said the villagers to one another, as they saw the familiar tall thin figure, black-garbed and grey-wigged, riding down the street on his stocky cob.

'Morning, your reverence!' they cried, and those with headgear tipped them while those without pulled their forelocks, and the parson in return raised his high-crowned hat.

No one noticed that ahead of the rider there flew a solitary magpie.

At about the time that his friends were setting out on their journey to find the parson, Tod woke, cramped and cold, on the hard wooden bench in the narrow dark cell. He had spent a mainly sleepless night, and now, in the chill light of dawn, his spirits were at their lowest ebb.

Would Matilda understand the message? Would help come? Would it come in time? Would he ever see any of his friends again, the four friends who had stood by him so loyally? He felt terribly alone, with now not even a familiar warm body in his pocket.

Time passed – oh, so slowly! – and then he heard a scrabbling noise and Evil re-entered the cell through the drain-hole. He looked very fat. His fur was draggled, and as he climbed on to Tod's lap, his normal smell, to which the toby man had long become accustomed, was overlaid by a much worse stink.

'Oh Evil!' said Tod. 'It's good to see you! Where have you been?'

'The answer is simple,' said the ferret in his thin scratchy voice. 'I have been making a tour of the town sewers. Full of rats, they are. But not quite as full as they were.'

Just then Tod heard the bolts of the cell door being drawn and the grate of the key in the lock, and he quickly put Evil in his pocket.

The turnkey came in.

'Come along o' me, boy,' he said.

'Where are you taking me?' said Tod fearfully.

'You'm to go before the Justices,' said the turnkey.

'Oh Lord-a-mussy!' whispered Tod.

'Ay,' said the turnkey, not unkindly, ''tis to be hoped He will.'

Chapter Twelve

Farewell to the Toby

The courtroom was packed.

All the townspeople had by now heard that a highwayman had been captured by the Bow Street Runners, and everyone who could came to see his trial, a trial that should by rights, they knew, end in a sentence of death. Those were cruel days, and most were looking forward not only to the proceedings but also in due course to the hanging, to the sight of a great hulking highway robber at the end of a rope.

All the more dramatic then was the sudden hush that fell upon the crowd as Tod was brought in and made to stand in the dock, facing the three magistrates. A highwayman! This gawky white-faced boy in the outsize fustian overcoat and the overlarge boots, who stood, dwarfed by the big turnkey standing behind him, and nervously twisted his tricorn hat in his hands! Why, he could not hold up a goat-cart, much less a stage-coach!

They settled down to listen.

The first. and as it happened the only witness, one of the Bow Street Runners, was called to the stand. He was the man who had sat upon Tod, the man whose bottom Evil had bitten, and he described the hold-up of the London-to-Bristowe stage-coach.

'I do not understand,' said the chairman of the Justices when the Runner had finished, 'why six men should have been sent to arrest one boy?'

'Well, your worship,' said the Runner, 'we was told as how there was a gang in Savernake Forest, three highwaymen, 'twas said, well-mounted and heavily-armed, with a pack of giant dogs.'

Some among the crowd began to laugh at the thought of such a force of men being employed to catch a ragged lad, but the chairman of the Justices called for silence in court.

'Know ye,' he said sternly, 'that this is no laughing matter. This youth is on trial for his life. To stop and rob a stage-coach on the King's highway is a capital offence, no matter the age of the culprit.'

At that point a tall thin black-clad figure rose at the back of the courtroom and said politely, 'May it please your worships, I should be obliged if you would permit me to comment in this case. It so happens that the accused, Tod Golightly, is a friend of mine.'

''Tis Parson Appletree,' someone said, 'from the village at the edge of the forest,' and the word went round, while in the dock Tod's white cheeks flushed and his heart began to hammer.

The Justices conferred together. Then they spoke.

'Your name, sir?'

'Parson Appletree.'

'And you tell us this lad is your friend?'

'I do.'

'And you have something to say on his behalf?'

'I have.'

'Pray continue, your reverence,' said the chairman of the Justices.

'I thank your worships,' said the parson.

He settled his grey wig more firmly on his head and, addressing the Runner, he said, 'You have told us that this boy stopped the stage-coach.'

'Yes, sir.'

'But the coach was already stopped. It was at a standstill, we are given to understand, so that the skid-pad might be fitted. No one, surely, can stop a coach that is already stationary?'

'Well, no sir, I suppose not,' said the Runner, 'but he had a blunderbuss. He was a-threatening us with a blunderbuss.'

'Unloaded, I believe?' said the parson.

'Well, yes sir, but he was planning robbery.'

'And what did he take?'

'Why, nothing.'

'He took nothing, but you, as you have stated, took from him a knife that you found upon him and the blunderbuss. Tod Golightly, it seems to me, was not the robber but the robbed.'

'He should not have been in possession of such a weapon, Parson Appletree,' said one of the Justices. 'For a boy to carry a gun and to point it at people – that is very wrong.'

'Very wrong indeed, your worship,' said the parson,

'and for that he should be punished. But I put it to you, gentlemen – boys will be boys. Whether they play at soldiers with wooden swords or at highwaymen with unloaded blunderbusses, they are but playing. Tod did not stop the coach. He did not rob the coach. He harmed no one. He merely pointed a gun that he should not have pointed, and for that behaviour you surely cannot exact the full penalty of the law. Punish him, yes, but temper justice with mercy.'

A loud murmur of agreement and applause ran round the courtroom, and calls of 'Well done, parson!' and 'His reverence is right!' were heard.

'Well, Mr Appletree,' said the chairman of the Justices, 'as you have argued so eloquently on your friend's behalf, perhaps you had better suggest the punishment. What do you consider would be fair?'

'A fine, your worships,' said the parson. 'A severe fine.'

'How much?'

'Three guineas, your worships. A great deal of money for such a lad.'

'It is indeed, sir. Severe is the word. It is a sum he could not possibly pay.'

'But I could,' said Parson Appletree. 'It just so happens that here in my purse,' and he produced it, 'are three guineas – a debt that I am due to repay. I should like, if you allow me, to pay it on Tod's behalf. And furthermore, I offer to make myself responsible for the lad's future behaviour, and indeed to take him to live under my own roof. Under my guardianship, I trust, he will come to see the error of his ways. For remember, your worships, and you good people all, the words of the Gospel. "Joy shall be in heaven over one sinner that repenteth, more than over ninety and nine just persons, which need no repentance."'

And, faced with such a sermon, and the whole-hearted agreement of the spectators, the Justices imposed the fine, and Tod was free to go.

As he turned to leave the dock, he happened to brush against the turnkey, and one of his hands happened to slip into the man's pocket.

So now the grey cob Martha trotted down the wide High Street, with Tod riding pillion behind the parson, and crossed the bridge over the river, and began the long climb up the steep curve of Forest Hill.

'Oh sir!' said Tod, when he had finished blurting out his heartfelt thanks, 'Am I really to come and live with you?'

'Only if you will give up your chosen profession, Tod.'

'Oh I will, I will!'

'And promise me never to steal again.'

Tod put his hand in the pocket of his old fustian coat and fingered the crown piece by which the turnkey was poorer. He sighed.

'No sir,' he said. 'Never again. It's the end of life on the toby for me, high or low. My mother will never see the gold coins and jewels and gems and pearls and precious stones that I boasted I would bring her. And I shall never see her again, I suppose.'

'Nonsense,' said Parson Appletree. 'She can come and visit you. I will see that she has the means to do so.'

'Oh thank you, sir!' cried Tod. 'That would be splendid. But what of all my friends? Can they stay?'

'The donkey I have met,' said Parson Appletree. 'A charming creature who would be such good company for Martha. They could stand head to tail in the hot summer days and flick the flies from one another, and in wintertime there is a spare loose box. Like me, she is no longer young, and indeed your legs will soon grow too long for you to ride upon her, but you will be welcome to a canter through the forest on Martha here whenever you wish. As for the mastiff – a noble fellow – he will guard us all against rogues.'

'Like highwaymen?' said Tod, grinning.

'Just so,' said the parson, straight-faced.

'And the magpie?' said Tod, pointing ahead at Loudmouth hunting the hedges.

The parson gave a special sort of whistle, and the bird immediately flew back and perched upon his shoulder.

'The magpie,' said Parson Appletree, 'is one of my favourite birds.'

He reached up and stroked the glossy head, and Loud-mouth gave a throaty chatter of delight before flying off again. She can have hours of pleasure, thought Tod, ferrying the rest of the money from the tree-hole.

'I have one more friend,' he said hesitantly. 'You have not met him.'

'Oh, where is he?' said the parson.

'Here,' said Tod, and he drew the ferret from his pocket and passed him to his new guardian.

'Whoa, Martha,' said Parson Appletree. He dropped the reins on her neck and taking Evil in one hand pulled his eyeglasses from his breast-pocket with the other and fitted them on the bridge of his nose. Short-sighted blue eyes peered into short-sighted red ones.

'The ferret,' he said, 'is one of my favourite beasts.'

'He's been down the sewers, rat-hunting,' said Tod apologetically.

'My sense of smell is not what it was,' said the parson. 'He will be of the greatest use to us. There are rats in the stable that eat Martha's corn and there are rabbits in the kitchen garden that eat my lettuces. But this fellow is no vegetarian. He must kill to live, it is Nature's way.'

He handed Evil back, took up the reins and clicked his tongue to the cob.

At the top of the hill, they turned off the road and struck across the forest, and before long they came

upon a herd of deer (which did not take fright at the sight of the parson, but stood and stared). Among them was a magnificent stag.

'What a splendid creature,' said Parson Appletree. 'I could never kill so fine an animal, could you, Tod?'

'Oh no!' said Tod. 'I couldn't.'

That's the truth, he said to himself, for I couldn't when I tried.

'But we will harden our hearts and kill a goose for Christmas,' said the parson, 'and Christmas will soon be here.'

'And,' he added, as they came to the edge of Saver-nake, 'we shall soon be home, shall we not, Martha?'

For answer the grey cob threw up her head and whinnied, and in reply they heard the bray of a donkey and the deep bark of a dog.

'Home!' said Tod wonderingly, as they clattered into the stable yard.

'Welcome!' said Parson Appletree.